Math Jokes Cheesy, and Clean Jokes For Kids and Math Teachers

By Andrew Howell

© Copyright 2018 by Andrew Howell - All rights reserved.

The following Book is reproduced below with the goal of providing information that is as accurate and reliable as possible. Regardless, purchasing this Book can be seen as consent to the fact that both the publisher and the author of this book are in no way experts on the topics discussed within and that any recommendations or suggestions that are made herein are for entertainment purposes only. Professionals should be consulted as needed prior to undertaking any of the action endorsed herein.

This declaration is deemed fair and valid by both the American Bar Association and the Committee of Publishers Association and is legally binding throughout the United States.

Furthermore, the transmission, duplication or reproduction of any of the following work including specific information will be considered an illegal act irrespective of if it is done electronically or in print. This extends to creating a secondary or tertiary copy of the work or a recorded copy and is only allowed with an expressed written consent from the Publisher. All additional rights reserved.

The information in the following pages is broadly considered to be a truthful and accurate account of facts, and as such any inattention, use or misuse of the information in question by the reader will render any resulting actions solely under their purview. There are no scenarios in which the publisher or the original author of this work can be in any fashion deemed liable for any hardship or damages that may befall them after undertaking information described herein.

Additionally, the information in the following pages is intended only for informational purposes and should thus be thought of as universal. As befitting its nature, it is presented without assurance regarding its prolonged validity or interim quality. Trademarks that are mentioned are done without written consent and can in no way be considered an endorsement from the trademark holder.

Table of Contents

Table of Contents

General Jokes 4
Math Movie Title Puns 27
Limericks 33
Calculus Math Jokes 41
Algebra Math Jokes 43
The Problem Around Light Bulbs 67
Number Math Jokes 74
Geometry Math Jokes 76
Statistics Math Jokes 78
Math Mistakes 86

General Jokes

3 Ft. of trash is called what?
A yard of junk.

To make 7 even, what do you do?
Take out the **S**

The girl wore glasses during her math session. Why?
It improved her **di vision.**

What made the math book super sad?
It had so many **problems.**

How are an empty parrot cage and a geometry shape similar?
Poly gon.

When dividing the diameter by the circumference of a pumpkin, what do you have left over?
Pumpkin pi

What makes trees hate doing math problems?
It makes their **roots square.**

Why did the boy consume his homework in math, prior to turning it in?
*Because his teacher said it was as easy as a **slice of pi.***

Do you think the latest statistics joke is a hoot?
Probably.

When the acorns grew up, what did they say?
Geometry

T'rex's favorite numeral is an?
8

Some snakes do great summation, which ones are they?
Add-ers

How does time fly?
You toss it out the window.

2 4's skipped lunch, what was their reason?
They had already 8.

Math instructor: What do you get with the problem 2 + 2?
Child: You get 4
Math teacher: That is great.
Child: Great? It is not great. It is perfect!

**Knock
Knock
Who is it?
Algi
Algi who?
Algi-bra**

The teacher wrote a math equation on the window. Why did he do that?
It needed to be clearer.

The Student said, "I know a joke about statistics."
*The Teacher said, "It's **Probably** a **mean** one"*

The student was multiplying her problems on the floor. Why did she do that?
*Her teacher asked her not to use **tables** to do the work.*

A mathematician's favorite dessert is what?
Math Pi.

The quarter did not roll down the mountain with the nickel, why is that?
*It was made up of more **cents**.*

Do you know a Math instructor's favorite season?
Summer time.

If a nose was 12-inches long what would it be?
A foot. It would be a foot

What happens when you blend a math instructor with an alarm clock?
Mathe ma ticks.

A number that cannot stand still, what is it?
It's a Roamin' numeral

If Matt, who has 60 cookies, eats 30 cookies. What does Matt now have?
A stomachache.

If caterpillars went to school, what class would they enjoy most?
Moth-ematics class.

The circle and rectangle were talking, what was said?
*How **square** can you be?*

If the pencil case was a kingdom who would be the king?
Duh, a ruler.

Students in class do not need to study which table?
The table they use for dinner.

The math book went to see a psychiatrist. What did he tell her?
I have so many problems, I need help.

If you mix a math instructor with a tree what is the result?
Math-ma- sticks.

The obtuse angle was super upset. Why was he upset?
It never was right.

The warlock was so bad at his math, why?
he was confused on Witch one of the Equations he needed to use.

The science book and algebra book were talking one day. The science book said to the algebra book, **"Geeze, I have way too many problems in my book."**

If the math book talked to the history book what would he say?
"Did you know that other people can count on you?"

There is only one number that cannot go down. What is it?
Someone's age.

There once was an old circle and a new square. One day they were talking, and the new square asked the old circle a question. He said, **"have you been 'round long?"**

The judge told the (6) and the (11) that they could not be married.
He said, "They were too young because they were under (18)".

What do you think is a heavier weight? 1-lb in feathers or 1-lb in cotton?
If they both weight the same, then neither one is heavier.

Why is the number (288) banned from the school building?
The principal says it is (2) gross. *(144 is considered a gross, 288 is 144 x2)*

The multiplication problem was eating breakfast. Which table did he use?
The times table.

The math book received low grades from the teacher.
He was cheating. Someone else did the problems for him.

If (1 = 5), (2 = 25), (3 = 125), and (4 = 525), then what does 5 equals?
(1)

What has too many problems and is the colors black and white?
The test in math.

Under the boy's pillow, he had a ruler. He said, "**he wanted to measure the length of his sleep time.**"

If the spelling book and math book talk, what do they say?
"I wish they could **count on you** like they do me."

Geometry asked the teacher, "why am I so adorable?"
The teacher told him, "You have some **acute angles.**"

"Answer this question quickly, when it is asked," said the teacher. What do you get when you add (5 + 3)?
"Quickly," I said.

If you have a need for 20-cents, how do you make it from 1 dime?
You stick it in front of your mirror.

There is only one table that you cannot eat at. What is it?
The table for multiplication.

The calculator told the girl, "**with me, you can solve all your problems.**"

Math problems can be solved with what part of your body?
The add-ums apple.

The right angle went swimming yesterday. How was the weather?
The weather was 90 degrees.

In 2008 how many women do you think where born?
Women are not born, only babies are.

How do inches follow each other?
With a ruler.

When you add 4 apples to 2 apples what would you get?
A math problem for a 2nd grader.

The girl was so angry with the math book that she yelled at it, ***"someday, I will stop solving your problems for you."***

Why do glue and math not go together?
Because the glue can get stuck in the problem.

Teachers in Maine love snacks. Which one is their favorite snack?
Whoopie Pi's

When you add a "g" to one, why does it vanish?
Because it becomes "gone"

Which tool is best used in Mathematics?
Multi pliers

The favorite tree of all math teachers is what?
Geo-ma-tree

The tangent line was talking to the circle. The tangent said, "***stop touching me.***"

Georgia teachers have a favorite dessert. Do you know which one it is?
Pi with a bit of peaches.

Why did the boy start to search after the terrible rain storm?
*Because the meteorologist said it had rain (1) inch and (3) quarters. and he wanted the **(3) quarters.***

Fractions are not always fraction's.
Because it they became a whole.

The more you remove from it the bigger it will be. What is it?
It is a hole.

I am removing (5) from the number (25). How many times can I do this?
One time. *After you take the first (5) you no longer have (25).*

I have $1 in my right pocket and $0.50 in my left pocket. How much do I have?
*The right amount for **buying some ice cream.***

I have (10) things that I can always count on. What do I have?
I have fingers.

If you mix a person with a calculator what do you have?
A person that can always be counted on.

If I have (20) things that I can use to count, what do I have?
*I have **ten fingers and ten toes**, that makes 20.*

(2) is company and (3) is a crowd, then what is (4) and (5)?
4 and 5 are 9.

In what way can a cow add?
*They can use a **cowwww-culator***

If you do mathematics in front of a lion, what do you get?
You get 8 because 4+4 equals 8

It's New Year's Eve, where are the math teachers going to celebrate?
Times Square

What did the cow do to reach the sum?
*He adds one number to **anudder one** and reaches a sum.*

Two friends, who love math are called what?
Alge-bros

A year has how many seconds in it?
(12), every month has a 2nd.

Why did (8) and (3) stop being friends?
(8) thought (3) was quite odd.

The chicken was crossing the Mobius strip.
He thought he should go to the other side.

How do you hit someone with a calculator?
By pushing the Cos Button

If you cross a math instructor with a clock what do you get?
Math ma ticks!

I dreamed that the world was weightless last night.
The world was (0)-mg.

If the chicken was to cross the Mobius strip what would it get?
*It would get to the exact **same side.***

New husband: How can you love math more than me?
New wife: I don't. I love you so much more.
New husband: I think you do, so prove it.
New wife: **then epsilon would be the greater of zero.**

Why did the Math instructor have a piece of graphing paper in class?
He must have been **plotting stuff.**

The other day Pi was arguing with the squared root of (2).
*They should stop being so **irrational.***

I heard the other day that there was a mathematical plant. Why is it so mathematical?
*It must be the **squared roots.***

If monsters were good at Mathematics, how many would there be?
*One when you **Count Dracula***

My bedroom is very cold. How do I get warmer?
*By going to the **90-degree** corner.*

The study of aliens has been taking place within the science community.

They found out that the **heights** *of aliens were* **distributed paranormally.**

The 4 was unable to enter the nightclub, but he did not know why?
He wasn't allowed because they thought he was **2 squared**

The student asked the math book, "Why are you so sad?"
The book responded, "because my problems are not solved."

An owls favorite style of Mathematics is what?
Owl Gebra

What happens to old math instructors?
They do not die, they just lose **functions.**

Once there was an English feline. His name was 1 2 3. Then he met a French feline. His name was un duex tres. One day they decided to race in order to see who would swim the English channel faster. Who do you think won?
Cats do not swim.

The calculator and the math instructor were talking one day. What do you think was said?
"I bet I can count on you."

If (**7 ate 9)**, then (6) would be afraid of (7).

If you place a Mathematics add in the paper, what will you get?
A mathematics Instructor.

Why did the student only complete (½) of his math homework?
He wanted to **prove** that he understood the work.

Why does a circle only have (2) sides to it?
Because it has the **outside and the inside.**

The student divided sin and tan. Why did they do that?
'Cos.

The obtuse triangle seems to be always upset. Why is that?
*Maybe it would like to be **right.***

Which (10) types of math instructors are there?
*The ones who are fluent in **binary** and the ones who are not.*

The math instructor proposed to his fiancée the other day. How did he do it?
*He used a **ring** that is **polynomial***

The (8) was incredibly happy when the (0) paid him a compliment. What did he say?
"You have a very nice-looking belt."

How many meals does a math instructor eat?
1 squared

Mathematics instructors love pumpkins on Halloween.
Because they can have their Pumpkin Pi.

Why was the algebra book so angry?
His **problems** were overwhelming.

What did the student say to the mathematics textbook?
*"Leave me alone, **I have too many problems of my own to deal with.**"*

The ghost was solving quadratic equations. How did he do it?
*He completed the **scare**.*

The mathematician was plowing the fields. What did he use?
*He used a **pro tractor***

The circle was doing flips one day. Why was he doing this?
*He wanted to get his **shape** back.*

I have heard that math instructors are good dancers. Why is that?
*They tend to have better **algo rhythm**.*

The first **sin**' of madness is using math puns.

Life would be **pointless** if it was not for geometry.

The math instructor was so tan that he became a **tan gent**.

Mermaids that attend math class have to wear what?
*They have to wear an **algae bra***

My **infractions** got me thrown out of math class one too many times.

My math instructor worships the **sum…**

Why did I study more geometry today?
*Because my math instructor told me I was out of **shape***.

The math instructor was unable to buy lunch today
*He was unable to **binomial**.*

Math instructors tend to be reluctant when they **cosine** for a loan.

If a math instructor is deaf how will he communicate to the class?
*With a language of **sine**.*

Old math teacher did not die. He had to **disintegrate.**

The mathematician was working at home. He was able to **function** better in his **domain**.

What is an **integral** part of doing **calculus**?
Finding **the area**.

One day the math instructor got tired of adding things up. What happened to him?
*He ended up in the hospital with an **incremental breakdown**.*

When I realize that **decimals** actually have a **point**, I started to love math.

My advanced geometry class is so boring. Why is it so boring?
*Because they are all **squares**.*

What did the arrogant math teacher do when he was wrong?
*He ate a slice of **humble pi.***

When math teachers retire, how do they **cope with the aftermath?**

I'm struggling in math class. It just feels like we are **going in circles.**

I only wear my glasses during math class. They improve my **di vision.**

Organic Math instructors are Earth conscious. ***They use Natural style logs.***

I may not like math, but I am very **partial** *to the* ***fractions****.*

I tried studying **negative numbers,** but I became nonplussed.

I read a math book the other day.
To be honest, I thought a lot of it was rather ***derivative.***

Schools never run out of their math instructors. Why is that?
Because they continue to **multiply.**

TEACHER: "What are (II) and (IV)?".
STUDENT: ***"Roamin' Numerals"***

How do you divide math instructors?

*By separating those that know **binary** from those that do not.*

What was the Tyrannosaurus Rex's favorite digit?
(8)!

What do you call elementary math snakes?
Adders!

Why did the (4)'s skip their lunch?
They (8) beforehand!

Martha has a son for every daughter she has. However, she only has seven daughters. How many children does Martha have?
Martha has (8) kids, one boy, and (7) girls.

What made the math textbook head to the hospital?
Its problems were overwhelming...

Which tables do children eat at?
Dinner tables.

What do you call a math student?
Multi-plyers.

What is (67 + 35 + 99 + 136 + 84)?
A headache.

How do you make one disappear?
By adding in G to the word one!

If two's company and three's a crowd, what are four and five?
Numbers

On a table there are (4) apples, you pick up (3) apples. How many apples do you now have?
(3)** because you only picked up **(3)

One day (2) sons went fishing with (2) fathers. They each caught one trout. How many fish did they have for dinner?
*They had **(3) fish** for dinner since the grandfather, Father, and son only caught one fish each.*

What is heavier? An ounce of sand or an ounce of rocks?
*They weight the same since they are both an **ounce**.*

The math textbook was so sad. He was tired of not solving his **problems**.

What US state has the most math teachers?
Mathachussets.

Why do teenagers travel in groups of (3) or (5)?
Because they can't even.

Why should you worry about the math teacher holding graph paper?
She's definitely plotting something.

Why did the math problem keep on moving?
Because it was roamin' numerals

What did one parallel line say to the other?
Fancy seeing you here.

Which monster is famous for doing Mathematics?
Count Dracula

You may think I'm **obtuse**, but that girl is **acute**.

*I can be a **numerator** and you can be a **denominator** and we can work together to lower ourselves to our **smallest forms**.*

"Hi, I hear you're good at algebra Will you **replace my X without asking Y?**"

I do not like my current girlfriend. Can I do a **substitution for y?**

Do you enjoy math and numbers?
Not really.
I don't either, but I do **care about your number.**

My last girlfriend is similar to **-1 square root, she is so imaginary.**

"You must be the square root of **-1 because you can't be real.**"

(0) is the derivative of my love, that means my love is **constant.**

You are a **function** that is **well-defined.**

I wish you were **derivative, that way I could lay tangent with your curves.**

To define our love, you would have to divide by **zero**. It simply cannot be done.

Love for another is a **positive function's concave first derivative**. It is always increasing.

If we are to study **non-Euclidean geometry,** then we would not be studying **Euclidian** style. Which means that we would not be parallel lines that do not touch.

Sometimes I feel irrational around you. You must be a square root of (2).

When I wrap my arms around you I feel **positive**, that must mean that you are a **modulus sine.**

Why is the obtuse angle so miserable?
*Because it cannot turn **right**...*

What's the best way to woo a math teacher?

*Use **acute angle**.*

Once there was a math instructor who had a terrible fear of negative numbers.

He stopped at doing nothing to stay away from the numbers.

How come old math instructors never die?

*They simply lose their **functions** first.*

My girlfriend is a (100) square root.

*She is purely imaginary but a **perfect (10)**.*

Math Movie Title Puns

The Bourne (Trig) Identity

Pi Hard

Sumdog Millionaire

Apo-cos-lypse Now

Factor the Future

Fatal Subtraction

An Officer and a Tan-gent-leman

Divide and Prejudice

Along Came Poly-gon

The radius of the Lost Arc

To Kill a Mocking Surd

(Rec)Tangled

Quadrilateral Damage

Mean Girls

Add Max

De-riving Miss Daisy

Sum Enjoy it Hot

Sin-set Boulevard

Gradients for the Galaxy

X (axis) Men

(Aste)Risky Business

What is the best angle to stay warm?
(90)-degrees Fahrenheit

What was the statistician saying about the math book?
It's Probable.

What's the best way to serve pi?
A la mode. **Anything else is mean.**

The farmer was counting his cows. He first found that he had (297) cows. Then he **rounded them up** and he had (**300**) instead.

Why did the statistician drown while crossing the River?
*He couldn't swim. The river had (**3**) **ft** of depth on* ***average.***

What stops a calculus major from going to a house party?
They do not want to ***derive.***

What made the cow go over the strip of Mobius?
He wanted to be able to stay in the **exact spot**.

Why does the math teacher love parks so much?
Because of all the **natural logs.**

How do you do math in your head?

*Just use **imaginary numbers.***

Why was the math conference so long?

*The professor kept going off on a **tangent.***

How many math teachers are needed for changing out the light bulb?

One—*the math instructor will turn the problem over to the physicist. The physicist will reduce the problem down to a solved problem.*

Why are math books so darn depressing?

*They're **literally filled with problems.***

Why does algebra make you a better dancer?

*Because you can use **algo-rhythm.***

What kind of snake does your math teacher probably own?

A pi-thon.

What's the best place to do math homework?
*On a **multiplication table**.*

How do you get from point A to point B?
*Just take an **x-y plane** or a **rhom'bus**.*

What did the student do to make 7 and even number?
*He removed the **"s."***

Where do math teachers like to party?
*In **bar graphs**.*

Why shouldn't you let advanced math intimidate you?
*It's really as easy as **pi**!*

What happens when you hire an odd-job guy to do (8) jobs?
*They only do **(1), (3), (5) and (7)***

What can you call nerds who love to do math together?

Alga bros.

Limericks

A math instructor excited
He learned the Mobius band is 1-sided
He knows you'll have an amazing laugh
When they cut one into two halves
Because it remains in 1 whole piece even when divided.

A math teacher called Klein
Decided he thought the Mobius group sounded divine
He exclaimed: If you use some glue
For the corners of the 2
You will receive a strange bottle similar to mine.

There was a super young boy called Fisk,
An expert with swords, exceptionally brisk.
So quick he was with actions,
The contraction of Lorentz
Lowered to a disk his rapier.

'Tis a wonderful assignment that is mine
A recent value that pi will assign.
It can be fixed at 3
For it seems easier, you'll see,
Than pi of 3.14159

If inside the circle there is a line
That hits the center of the circle and goes from spine to spine
And the length of the line represented by "d"
then those circumferences should also be
d multiplied by pi of **3.14159**

Pi goes on with no end ...
And **e** can seem just as cursed.
I wonder often: Which one is much larger
When those digits reverse?

A competition that took place for many long ages
Was baffling to the genius as well as those sages
Yet suddenly there was light:
I guess the old Fermat was exactly right--
To every single margin, he included (200) pages.

In tropical and arctic climes,
within those integers, additions, and times,
taken of the mod **p** they will yield
an entire field of the finite,
Ranges that stretch of the **p**.

A student who graduated from Trinity
Calculated the cubes with which were infinity;
however, this caused him to fidget
To jot these down in digits,
So he stopped doing the math and started with divinity.

In all situations, the prime is in the middle of **2n and n.**

Three people discussed which was better, a girlfriend or a wife. One was a physicist. The other was a computer scientist. The last one was a Mathematician. The Physicist stated, "A girlfriend. You will still have the freedom you need to experiment." The suddenly the Mathematician exclaimed, "A wife. You will have a ton of security." Then the Computer Scientist expressed, "Both. When I am at work my wife thinks I'm with the girlfriend and the girlfriend thinks I'm with the wife. I'm rarely with either, most the time I'm at my computer not being disturbed by either."

One mathematician, one scientist, and one engineer go on a vacation together. They are driving through the countryside when suddenly the car stops running. Although the countryside is nice they need to continue on their drive. The mathematician suggests heading back to the gas station they passed a few minutes ago. The engineer suggests that he should take a look at the car first. Thinking he can possibly fix it. The computer scientist suggests opening all the doors, slamming them shut and then checking to see if the car reset.

Young Child: "My math teacher is crazy." Boy's Mom: "Why?" Young child: "Yesterday she told us that **five is (4+1); today she is telling us that five is (3 + 2)."**

"What happened to your girlfriend, that really cute math student?" said the kids best friend. "She no longer is my girlfriend. I caught her cheating on me," said the kid. "I don't believe that she cheated on you!" Exclaimed the best friend. *"Well, a couple of nights ago I called her on the phone, and she told me that she was in bed wrestling with three unknowns..."* remarked the kid.

The parent is extremely disappointed in her child's functions.
*She has reached the anger **limit.***

What was the math teachers rating for the movie American Pie?

3.14

(6) are no longer friends with (7).
Ever since (7 8 9)

The math instructor told the kids at his table during Christmas dinner, root-1/root 64. What was he saying?
1 over 8

An artificial tree for Christmas is similar to the 4th root of -68. How is that?
*Neither of them has **real roots.***

Why did seven eat nine?

*Every day you must **eat (3) square meals a day**.*

The Romans did not find algebra too challenging.

*Because the Romans already knew **x was equal to (10)**.*

Why are math parties held without drinks?
*So they do not **drink and then derive.***

What is a girl's favorite ring?
*The diamond **polynomial ring!***

Take a math instructor and cross it with a crab. What do you get?
Answers that are snappy.

Identify the difference between a large pizza and a Ph.D. in mathematics?
Large pizzas will feed a family of more than (3).

How does a Math Instructor demand positive behavior in her kids?
N times to infinity

The accumulation point that is the largest of the poles is what?
Warsaw!

What voice message will you hear when you get your math instructors voicemail?
"This number is imaginary if you have dialed it then rotate the phone in a 90-degree angle and try that number again."

What is complete, yellow, and normed?
*A **space Bananach.***

What did (2) tell (4) after (2) placed 1st in the race?
I am (2) Fast (4) U!

How was Al gore able to play his guitar?
*He had **algo rhythm!***

What did the math instructors parrot chirp?
I am a poly "no meal"

What is the reason for people to put the numbers (2), (3), and (0) together?
*Because they are **two turdy.***

Why did the one math book get so mad at the other math book?
*Because he was causing him to have more **problems**.*

How do you define a polar bear?
*A bear that's rectangular after it has a **transformation coordinate***

She wanted a calculator, she got my **log** with a **natural rhythm**.

MATH stands for **Mental Abuse To Humans.**

Dear Math, I am not a Counselor… can you please, **solve your own stupid problems now**.

There are three people, who apply for the same job. Each one brings something to the table. The interviewers on the committee call the math teacher in. They ask, "We only have the one question. What is 500 + 500?" The math teacher does not hesitate, and answers "1000." The interviewers thanked him and sent him on his way. Then they asked the statistician to come in. They proceed to ask him the same question. The statistician considers this question for some time, and then she answers "1000… I'm confident 95% that this is correct." The interviewers again thanked her for her time and sent her on her way, as well. They call the accountant into the room, They proceed to ask him the same general question, "What is 500 + 500?" The accountant asks, "**What do you want it to be?" As they talk it over they decide the accountant is the one to hire.**

Father: "What did your teacher teach you in school today?" Son: "We played a game where we were guessing!" Father: "I thought your math exam was scheduled for today?" **Son: "Exactly!"**

Two men that are statisticians have gone bird hunting in the woods. The first one fires and just barely missed by shooting

(5) ft. past the bird. The second one fires and just barely misses by shooting (5) ft. shorter than the bird. They both look at each other and get excited. They give each other a high five and exclaim. **"Got it."**

When the angle wanted to get a loan, what was stopping him?

*His parents refused to **Cosine**.*

*The math book was visiting the counselor. She asked why are you so sad? He replied "My **book is full of problems**.*

The obtuse angle went to the beach the other day.

*He wanted to enjoy the **90-degree** weather.*

What is an acute angle?

An angle that is adorable.

Why does no one communicate with circles?

*Because they make no valid **points**.*

Calculus Math Jokes

"Sketching rational functions is a pain in the **asymptote!**"

Why isn't the sociologist differentiating?

*Because the sociologist is without **a function.***

Bob had a glass of water and (8) pieces of ice in it. Why did he not drink it?

*He thought it was too **cubed**.*

Why were tan and sin not invited to party with the others?

The other people had cos

What is the reason why decimals always win an argument?

They always have a valid point.

What do you call a number that is from Rome?

A Roamin' numeral.

Dear Algebra, Do not ask me to find your X anymore.
*She does not want to come back—**I do not know Y.***

The witch doctor has a curse removal formula. What does he call it?

Hex a gon.

The roundtable was invented by who?
Sir Cumference.

Algebra Math Jokes

When 4 and 4's lunch time arrived, they refused to go. Why do you think they did that?

They thought they 8 already

The teacher called the student average, and he got upset. Why do you think this is?
He thought she was being 'mean'

Three statisticians are sitting in the woods hunting rabbits. They soon see a rabbit by itself. They each take aim and the first one misses by overshooting. The second one misses by undershooting. The third one yells, **"We got him"**

Two variables, that are random, were speaking at the snack bar. They believed they were not being loud, but we all could hear the chatter that was continuous.

The statistician that was crossing the river, was worried he would drown. The river was (3) ft in depth on average.

Write this expression to get the volume of a pizza crust that is thick using height "a" and radius "z".
The answer is pi·z·z·a

"What is the integral of 1/cabin?" "log cabin." "No, you must have forgotten the C. Houseboat $\int(1/\text{cabin}) = \log_e(\text{cabin}) + c$*, or "a log cabin + the sea"*

How many math instructors should it take to insert a new light bulb?
One but they need 3 physicists to assist.

Three scholars are watching a house from across the street while sitting on the bench. They notice that 2 people walk into the house. Then a bit later (3) more people come from inside the house. One of the scholars, who is a physicist, exclaims, "the measurement initially was incorrect." The other one, who is a biologist remarks, "They must have reproduced." The last one, who is a math instructor then explains, "If exactly one person enters that house, it will be empty."

Several math teachers walk into the soda shop. The first one asks for a soda. The second one asks for (½) a soda. The third one asks for (¼) of the soda. The server brings back 2 sodas. The math instructor asks if that is all they get. The server replies that those are there limits.

Several Math instructors walk into the soda shop. The first will order one full root beer. The second one will order ½ root beer. The third one will order a ¼ of a root beer. Then the

Manager of the soda shop yells, "Get out of here are you trying to shut me down?"

When a statistician enters the security check at the airport, the security officers find a bomb located in his bags. The statistician begins to explain. "Statistics shows that the probability of a bomb being on an **airplane is 1/1000. However, the chance that there are two bombs on one plane is 1/1000000.** So, I am much safer..."

What will happen when a mosquito crosses with a mountain climber?
Not one thing. It is impossible to cross a scalar with a vector.

One decimal said to the other decimal, did you understand my **point**?

Math Instructors have been climbing trees for a long time. Which one would they climb?
The geoma tree

My sister was walking around the house with a piece of graphing paper. She must be working on a new **plot**.

*If **(6 out of 5) people** struggle with fractions? Does that mean that (3 out of 2) are mathematicians?*

Why did the (4) turn away from the geometry club?
Because he was just too square.

What made the math book happy?
*His **problems** were being solved.*

*Where do old math teachers go when they lose functions? The operating **tables**.*

What do you call Math parents?
***Multi-plyers**.*

How do you locate a math tutor?
*Place an **add!***

*The student was so excited that he understood the class work that he did **(1/16)** of the problems.*

The most famous King in Europe invented fractions.
*Who was **Henry the 8th***

Which side will a circle take in an argument?
*The **inner or the outer***

Why would you divide sin by tan?
Cos

What does (01134) spell on the calculator?
HELLO

The other day the #6 was playing hide and seek with the sq. root of -1. *It was cute that he had an **imaginary friend.***

Why did the mother find her daughter doing her math homework in the bath?
*Because her teacher asked them not to use the **tables**.*

There are (2) types of Math Instructors.
Those that can screw in a light bulb and those that ask the physicist.

*The fiancée was so mad at her boyfriend that she threw her **polynomial ring** right back at him.*

What do you call children that add up math equations?
Adders

Why did the tier not work?
Because it was square.

Why was the math instructor so angry?
Because his student wouldn't stop going off on tangents.

It takes **50% of your imagination** to understand a simple math equation.

"A mathematician is a device for turning coffee into **theorems**"

If his equations approximate reality, then he must be an engineer. If reality approximates his equations, then he must be an engineer. If you do not care, then you must be a **mathematics teacher.**

Math teachers are like men from France: no matter what it is you said to them, they will translate those words into their **own language**.

Mathematics the art of calling different things by the same name.

*Why is the common definition of the word rigor, **rigorous**?*

*There is no absolute foundation of **math** that is logical, **and** Gödel has proven this to be so!*

If she does not think, would she really be?

A math instructor is like a man that is blind and lost in a dark room. This man is searching for the only cat that is black in the room. Only thing, is the black cat is no longer there.

If you lack in personality but are good with numbers, what are you?
*A **statistician***

*The universe cannot be classified as banana and non-banana just like the Math problem cannot be **linear or non-linear.***

*To prove a result that is deep, there is no absolute way that it can be done. That is why we use the **law of conservation for difficulties**.*

A conjecture that is beautiful yet ruined by ugly facts is a tragedy of mathematical proportions.

If you do not understand what you are talking about, use an Algebraic symbol.

Philosophy is a process where you have a goal without guidelines.

Mathematics is a process with lots of guidelines and absolutely no objectives.

Math along with love can both be a simple idea, however, math is much more complicated.

How are Math and checkers similar?
They are both not too difficult to grasp, they are suitable for all ages, they are both amusing, and you can do both of them without peril to your state.

An introverted math teacher will stare at the ground, while an extroverted will look everywhere but directly at you.

Zeus is real unless he is a proclaimed **integer.**

Mathematics makes people sad, Medicine makes people ill and Theology makes people sinful.

If you can properly define, then divide, then you must be a genius.

Physicists will delay only with a math teacher; math teachers will delay only with God.

If jokes about trigonometry are overly graphical, and jokes about algebra are overly formulaic, and jokes about arithmetic are overly basic, and jokes about calculus are completely derivative, then that is the problem with a math pun. The occasional statistics joke is outer.

The irrational fear of convergent sequences is **Xenophobia**

My statistics class is so long, that if I was living for only 24 hours I would rather spend it in this statistics class.

A Mathematician and Physicist are discussing putting out a fire. The physicist suggests using a bucket of water. The mathematician says he will just hand his bucket to his physicist friend. This will eliminate the situation down to the previous problem which is solved.

Stranded on a deserted Island, the math teacher and the engineer try to figure out what they need to do now. The Engineer decides to climb up a coconut tree and collect the only coconut from that tree. He then opens it and eats it. The Math teacher also climbs up a tree. However, he chooses the other tree. Then he grabs that one coconut and climbs all the way to the second tree and places it on it. "**Now they have reduced it so that they have an easier problem to solve.** "

Two people walk into a building, only to leave ten minutes later with 3 people in the group.
"They have multiplied," said the biologist.
"Oh no, it's an error in measurement," the physicist sighed.
"If one person is to enter the building, then it will likely be empty once again," concluded the math instructor.

A mystic, physicist, as well as a mathematician, were asked what the best inventions were of all time. The Physicist thought for a bit and chose fire. Because with fire we have power over matter. The Mathematician thought for a bit longer and he chose our alphabet. Because with the alphabet we are able to have power over symbols. The Mystic thinks for even longer and decides that the thermos bottle was the best. The other people asked, "Why a thermos bottle?" So, the Mystic explains, "Because the thermos keeps hot liquids hot in winter and cold liquids cold in summer." The scientist asks, "Yeah, so what?" "Think about it." said the Mystic earnestly. **"That little thermos bottle, how does it *know* what to do?"**

Three men are stranded on an island. One chemist, one math teacher, and one physicist. They are sitting on the island and a can of food just rolls up. They do not have a can opener, so they are puzzled on how to open the can. As they sit there thinking about it the Math teacher gets a brilliant idea and says, **"Let's just assume that we already have a can opener."**

A Math instructor was asked to create a kitchen table. His first attempt at the design had no legs. The second table he creates has a number equal to infinite, of legs. Then he proceeds to spend the majority of his whole life contemplating the answer to this kitchen table build as **N equals 0 legs**. Where N cannot be a number that is natural.

One day there was a panel of scientists who were asked to answer a question: "What is pi?" As the Engineer contemplated on the answer he finally said, "It is approximately 3 and 1/7." The Physicist thought really hard and then said, "It is 3.14159" The Mathematician contemplated the same question and decided to say, "It is equal to pi". Then a nutritionist walks by and replies, **"Pie is a healthy and delicious dessert!"**

A weapons Engineer, a Physics instructor, and a Math instructor were traveling across Scotland on a train. Sudden they pass by some sheep in a field. They identified the sheep as being black. "Aha," the Engineer says, "I see that all of the Scottish sheep are black." "Hmm," the physicist says, "You mean that some of the Scottish sheep are black." **"No," exclaims the math teacher, "All we know is that there is at least one sheep in Scotland. That one sheep is at least black on one side."**

An Engineer, Math teacher, and Scientist are all asked, "What if we defined a horse's tail as a leg. How many legs would a horse have then?" The math teacher answers with **"5"; the scientist responds with "1"; and as the engineer contemplates he says, "But you are not able to do that."**

One Engineer, one Math teacher, and one Physicist are all given a ball made of rubber that is identical and told to find the volume of the ball. The participants can use as much time as they need and any tool they want to reach their answers. The math teacher gets his measuring tape and proceeds to write down the circumference of the ball. He starts to divide that by 2 x pi, which gives him the radius of the ball. He then multiplies the number to the 3rd and proceeds to multiply by pi again. Next, he proceeds to multiply this number by 4/3 and finally derives the volume. The physicist then decides to get a large bucket and uses 1 gallon of liquid to fill the bucket. He then proceeds to drop the ball into the bucket. He uses the displacement to measure the ball up to 6 figures that are significant. **The engineer believes himself to be smart, so he simply writes down the number associated with the products serial #, which is on the packaging, and searches for it on the online specs. page.**

A Math teacher and his friend who is an Engineer attends a lecture where the guest speaker was a special Physicist. The topic they were discussing was the theories of Klein. This strongly involved processes that are physical, which can occur in the spaces that preside within the dimensions of 9 and even higher than 9. The Math instructor is lounging on the chair and is showing clear signs that he is enjoying the lecture. The engineer, on the other hand, is frowning and looks unhappy about the lecture. He does not understand the contents. By the end of the lecture, the Engineer is suffering from a throbbing headache. The Math teacher exclaims that he fully enjoyed the lecture and that he found it quite wonderful. The Engineer looks at him in a bewilderment, "How did you understand this lecture?" the Mathematician excitedly says, "I just used a visualization process." The engineer looks at him and states, " It's in 9-dimensional space how can you POSSIBLY visualize something that occurs there?" **It's easy, first you visualize it in N-dimensional space, and then you let the N go to 9",** says the Math teacher.

A team of engineers assembled to measure the height of the flagpole at a school. The engineers were required to use only a tape measure. They were getting overly annoyed as they tried to keep the measuring tape in place alongside the pole and it would not stay. They were agitated since it kept falling down. A math teacher walks by and asks the others what the problem is. They proceed to explain the situation and the Math teacher asks why they did not take the pole from inside the ground in order to measure it that way. When the math teacher leaves, one of the engineers says to the other: **"Just like a math teacher! We needed to know what the height is, and he gave us directions on how to get the length!"**

A farmer asked one day if a math teacher, an engineer, and a physicist could build a fence to fence off the largest area of square feet possible, but using the least amount of fence available, for a fence on his property. The engineer designed his fence in an exact circle and explained how his design was the best way to efficiently use the materials. Next, the physicist builds a straight line of fence as far as the eye can see and explains, "they can assume that the length of the fence is infinite." he then points out that he is fencing (1/2) of the earth off and that it was a more useful way to fence off the building. The math teacher just starts laughing at them. He starts to build a tiny circle shaped fence around his current space and declares, **"I have placed myself on the outside of the fence."**

A physics teacher and his friend the engineer decide to take a ride on a hot air balloon. Soon they start to travel along. Soon they find that they have become lost in the canyon. They get worried and yell out trying to get help: "Hello! Where are we?" about (15) minutes pass by and the friends hear a voice that echoes: "you are here." and the physicist says, "That must have been a math teacher." Even though the engineer agrees with his friend, he asks "Why do you say that?" His physics friend chuckles and replies: "The answer was absolutely correct, as well as, **utterly useless."**

A Dean of students is addressing the heads of the Department of Physics at his University, "Why do I always have to give you guys so much money. You all need so much money for expensive equipment, laboratories. Why couldn't you be like the Math Department? They only need money for pencils, paper, and waste-paper baskets. Or the Philosophy Department, all **they use are pencils and paper."**

One day a math Instructor, a chemist, and an engineer decided to take a walk down the street. On the side of the road, they noticed a pile of soda cans. Since these were the old-style cans they did not have a pull tab. They decided to go back to their respective labs and design something to open the cans. The chemist made a chemical that magical dissolves the top of the can instantly, without affecting the soda. The engineer designed a new Hyper Opener, which opens 25 cans per second. When the two returned to the cans, they were confident in the new inventions. They saw the math teacher sitting there drinking the very last soda. Puzzled they asked the man, "How did you manage that?" The math instructor answered, **"Oh, I assumed that they were already open and went from there.**"

At the local airport, an accomplished math teacher from a local high school was arrested today for attempting to board a flight.

He had his protractor, his compass, and his graphical calculator. The airport security believed that he had ties to the Al-Gebra network. The math teacher received a citation by the airport security for withholding some weapons that had math instruction They also believed that he was helping **students solve problems with help from some radicals!**

A man wins some money from the lottery where his prize is defined as infinite amounts of hundreds. He is rather jubilant until he finds out how much he has won. When he learned of the payment mode, he learns he will earn, **$1 now, $0.50 next week, $0.27 the week after that...**

One math teacher, one Engineer, and one Physicist are placed in individual rooms. Each room only contains 3 spheres made of metal and a table. The spheres are softball size. They are each told to do what they want with the balls within a one-hour period. The Math teacher arranged the metal balls into a triangle. The Physicist arranges them into a stack, with one on top of the other. The Engineer has **one ball broken, one is missing and the other one is in his lunchbox when he exits the room.**

One day a math teacher makes a choice to learn more about equations that are practical. He attends the conference, with a title that is seemingly nice: **"The Theory of Gears." So, the Math teacher decides to attend it. When the lecture starts the guest, speaker stands up and starts his speech saying, "The theory of gears with a real number of teeth is well known ..."**

The white house check notices that the statistician that is passing through has a bag with a bomb inside. He tries to explain by saying, "Statistics indicates that with the probability of a bomb being on the property **is 1/1000**. However, the chance that there are two bombs within one day **is 1/1000000.** So, I am much safer..."

What is different with a Neurotic, a Math teacher and a Psychotic? The Psychotic will fully believe in himself being correct by saying (2+2=5). A Neurotic fully knows that the correct answer is ***(4=2+2), however, it will kill him to know this. A math teacher will simply alter the base of the equation.***

Which one do you think the logician will choose: a (1/2) of the egg or bliss for eternity in his afterlife?
(1/2) of the egg! *As he knows that absolutely nothing would be a better choice than bliss for eternity in the afterlife, and a (½) of an egg is better than absolutely nothing.*

An Engineer and a Mathematician were confined in two separate rooms for an entire day. They were given some food to eat but they were not given anything to open it with. When the day ended the Engineer was found sitting in the floor with the open can, eating the food. He had thrown the can against the wall until it opened. The mathematician was nowhere to be found, although the can is still in the room. Suddenly they hear strange noises coming from the can and out pops the mathematician. The Mathematician says, "**Man! I got a sin' wrong.**"

*Pure mathematicians are like lighthouses in the **middle of a swamp** — brilliant, but completely useless.*

I'm not worried about losing my job to a computer. They have yet to invent the machine that does absolutely nothing.

For every mathematical problem that is complex, there is an elegant and simple solution that is totally wrong.

For every complex mathematical problem, there is a solution. The difficulty lies in finding it.

A mathematics lecture is a process for translating the notes that your teacher has given you into notes that you can use for studying without entering the mind of either person.

Statistics are like a bikini — **what is concealed is vital, however, what they reveal is quite suggestive.**

If you get depressed when you consider how dumb the common person is... then you are horrified to realize that ($½$) **the world's population are even dumber.**

Light can travel faster than the speed of sound, which is the reason why some people will appear brighter until you hear them talk.

People who take a long time **computing the ratio of rising to run are slope pokes.**

Just because you attended school does not qualify you to teach, any more than being in a carport means you can call yourself a car.

Mathematicians don't suffer from insanity. They enjoy every minute of it!

The derivative of my enthusiasm for mathematics is positive for all values of the **independent variable.**

Whenever *4 math teachers get together*, you'll likely find a fifth.

"Take a positive integer n. No, wait, n is too large; take a positive **integer k.**"

To a math teacher, finding solutions means finding the answer. **But to a chemist, the solutions tend to be things that will still be quite mixed up in the end.**

The enthusiasm a professor has for teaching **pre-calculus can vary inversely** due to the likelihood that the actually has to do it.

Two male math teachers are in a bar. One of the men argues that non-mathematicians probably know very little basic math. The other guy disagrees, claiming that most people have a reasonable amount of math skills. The first guy gets up and heads to the bathroom, while the other one calls over the waitress. He explains to her that once his friend returns to the table he will call her over and ask her a question. He proceeds to tell her that she only needs to answer the question with 1/3x cubed. She replies with, "one thir -- dex cue"?

He repeats "1/3x cubed". Her: `one thir dex cubed'? Yes, exactly, says the guy. The server agrees and as she walks away she goes over the words aloud, so she can remember, "one their dex cubed". When the other man comes back from the bathroom, the other one proposes that they ask the waitress some questions on integrals and prove a point about the argument. The other guy laughs and then takes the bet. So, they call the waitress over to ask her, "what is the integral of x squared?". The waitress confidently replies, "one-third x cubed" then proceeds to walk away, slowly she looks over her shoulder and adds, "**plus a constant!**"

A math teacher, who was a Texan, found himself asked by his class, "What are mathematics good for?" He then responded with, "That question makes me sick." "If somebody asks you what the Grand Canyon is good for, the first time they see it," "What would you do?" Then he responds, **"Probably kick them off the cliff, right?"**

A future society has started selling pills designed to advance your knowledge of basic subjects. One day a student goes to the pharmacology and questions the pharmacologist about which type of educational pills he had in stock. The pharmacologist states, "We have a pill for English literature." The student then buys the pill and immediately swallows them. Instantly gaining all the knowledge about English Literature. Then the student asks, "what other pills are available?" "Well, I have pills for world history, art history, as well as biology." says the pharmacist. The student then purchases all of them and immediately swallows the pills. He instantly is able to gain knowledge about all of those subjects. Now the student is considered an advanced learner. The student then asks, "What about a pill for math?" The pharmacist says, "Hold on," and heads back to the storage room only to return with this gigantic horse pill that is super heavy. "That is the pill for math?" the student inquiries. The pharmacist laughs and then replies *"Yes. Math always was a little bit harder to swallow."*

The well-known rule for any instructor of math: **We should all tell the truth, and not anything else, except the truth, but never the whole truth.**

A math professor tends to talk in **another person's sleep.**

If you add (2) apples with (3) apples what do you get?

A math problem from high school.

Teacher: The number of sheep that you have available is defined by x...
Student: Yes sir, but what will happen with the sheep if the number is **not really x?**

The child said, "There are (4) airplanes that are flying in the sky. Then (2) added airplanes start to fly by. How many of the airplanes do you see that are flying around now? The Father was confused and disappointed that his son could not grasp this problem of the simplest form. "What confuses you, son?" the father asked. The child puzzled, responds: *"I know, that*

(4 + 2=6), but what I haven't figured out is what the airplanes have to do with this!"

The guest speaker at the college tells some of the student body to remember the phone-book by heart.
The math students are quite baffled: `Are you kidding?
The students in physics ask: `Why would I want to do that?'
The engineers loudly sighed: `Do we really have to remember that?'
The students of chemistry ask: 'By Monday of next week?'
The students of accounting (jotting notes in their books) respond: `We will have it sometime tomorrow?'
The students of law answer: `We have already.'
The students of the medical school responded with: `**Should we begin with the Yellow Pages?'**

"The problems located in the exam will be similar to the ones we discussed in class previously. Of course, the numbers will be different. But not all of them. *Pi will still be 3.14159...* "

*"Roses are red,
Violets are blue,
Greens'* **functions are boring**
And so are **Fourier transforms**."

There are 3 types of students in this world; **those who count and those who do not know how to count**

There are (10) kinds of people in the world, those that understand how to do **the binary math, and those that do not understand binary math.**

There are (2) distinct types of mathematicians in this world. The ones that **do not do the math, and the ones that do and take care of those who do not.**

"The world is **dense with idiots,** everywhere."

How can you tell that you have joined forces with the Math Mafia?
Their offer is something you just do not understand.

What has a cherry pit inside and is small, red, and round?
A cherry.

An insane math teacher begins threatening everyone when while on the bus, "I'll integrate you! I'll differentiate you!!!" Everyone gets scared and they proceed to run away. One lady stays behind. The guy goes to speak to the lady and asks: "Aren't you scared, I'll integrate you, I'll differentiate you!!!" The lady calmly answers him*: "No, I am not scared, I am e^x."*

"The number you have dialed is imaginary. Please rotate your phone **90 degrees** and try again."

*let epsilon mean < **0***

How often can you take (7) from the number (83), and what is remaining?
*I can **subtract it repeatedly, and it will continue to have remainders of (76) every time**.*

Why was the Moebius strip not allowed to enroll at the school?
The school's orientation was a requirement for him.

What song is the longest in the world?
*"**Aleph naught** cans of pop on the Wall."*

Why does the technology scientist get the holiday Halloween and Christmas all scrambled?
He knows that (10+31=12+25)

Why would the chicken pass through the Mobius strip?
To move to the opposite ... err, um ...

What happens when you mix the banana and an elephant?
| banana |*| elephant | * **sin(theta)**

If you blend a mosquito and a climber of mountains what is left?
*It is not advisable to cross a **vector and a scalar.***

2 instructors of math are studying convergent in a series. The first guy says: "Do you understand that the series converges even when all the terms are made positive?" The second guy asks: "Are you sure?" **"Absolutely!"**

Life is more complex than you know: it is filled with equal parts of the ***imaginary and the real components.***

"Divide (14) sugar cubes into (3) cups of coffee so that each cup has an odd number of sugar cubes in it." "That's easy: one, one, and twelve." "But twelve isn't odd!" *"**Twelve is an odd number of sugar cubes** to place in his cup of coffee..."*

A statistician** will exclaim that on average he feels fine, but* ***he often has his feet in ice and head in the fire.

The Problem Around Light Bulbs

Calculate the number of math instructors it will take to screw that light bulb in?
A math instructor is not able to screw the light bulb in, but he is easily able to prove that the light bulb problem exists.

How many math instructors will it involve for you to screw in the light bulb?
One math instructor. *Since he will give it to (4) computer programmers, thereby reducing the problem to one that is solved.*

What is the number of math instructors it takes to screw in a light bulb?
*The sum is **obvious, intuitively***

How many math instructors will it take to get that light bulb screwed in?
*In Wieners earlier work, he found that **one math instructor could change a light bulb.***

What number of math logicians do you need to put in a new lightbulb??
o can do it

How many number analysts will it take to put in a lightbulb??
after the 6th iteration 3 and .9967

How many geometers which are classical, will you need to place a new lightbulb?
None: *They are not able to do it while using a straight edge or compass.*

How many constructivist math instructors does it take to put in a new lightbulb??
0: *They have no belief in rotations that are infinitesimal.*

The situationists are in the room needing to replace the lightbulb, questioning how many it will take.
Infinitely more than they know: *Each one will build a fully validated model, but the light will never materialize.*

Then topologist wonder how many of them can change one lightbulb?
They only need one. *But, they all wonder what will happen with the doughnut?*

How many analysts will you need to replace a lightbulb??
Three: *One to prove that the light bulb exists, one to prove the uniqueness of the light bulb, and one to derive the algorithm that is nonconstructive in order to complete the action.*

If you have (10) professors, who many are needed to change the light bulb?

One: With (8) students who are researching, (3) post-docs, (2) programmers, and a secretary that will help him.

The room is full of lecturers from the University and they want to know how many will be needed to change the light bulb?
4: (1) to change it and (3) to help with the research paper as co-authors.

If you have X to represent graduate students and Y to represent light bulbs, how many of X does it take to solve Y's problems?
Only one is represented by X: however, you will wait (9) years to get there.

How many administrators from the university math department will be needed to change the lightbulb?
No one will change it, because they do not see the problem with the old one.

Puns

What is a circle's area?
pi R^2?

Pi is not a square. Pi is round. **Cornbread can be square.**

What is a dilemma?
A lemma that presents a problem.

What lives in the sea and is non-orientable?
Mobius Dick.

What commutes and is the color purple?
A grape abelian.

What is a polar bear in math terms?
*A bear **that is rectangular** after it has been transformed by a coordinate.*

*Many people suggest that the new Pope will be one of the **best cardinals.***
But other people dictate that it simply is not true, because all the popes have had great successors.

Can a lightbulb change another light bulb?
Yes, one will do it as long as it knows its own Goidel #.

What clothing can you see the little mermaid wearing?
Algae bras

Was Coronel **Calculus** a hero of the Roman war?

"What's your favorite thing about mathematics?" **"Knot theory."** "Yeah, me neither."

What stopped Newton from being able to discover the theory of groups?
*He simply wasn't **Abel.***

In the state of Alaska, ***Eskimo pi*** is what you get when pi gets super cold. As with everything else when pi gets cold it drops to 3.00 because could makes everything shrink.

In (3) steps I will prove that a piece of paper is also a lazy dog.
1. ***A piece of paper can be called an ink-lined plane.***
2. ***An inclined plane can be called a slope up.***
3. ***A slow pup can be called a lazy dog.***

*A math teacher visited the beach to sunbath, he soon became a **Tangent.***

Student: Teacher, I am unable to solve this equation.
Teacher: Any 5-yr. old can solve this equation.
Student: No wonder I am unable to, I am ten!

Teacher: How many have parents that helped with the homework assignment?
Pupils: None, we got all the answers wrong on our own.

Who was the inventor of algebra?
A clever X-pert.

What does a fisherman use to determine the amount of cod he needs to catch in order to make a profit?
He needs an **inequality cod ratic.**

What steps does the ghost use to complete an equation of quadratics?
*He has to complete the **scare.***

Teacher: What is the answer to (2) n plus (2) n equal too?
Student: I am not sure. It **all sounds completely foreign to us.**

What was the reason why the math tree fell to the ground?
It roots happened to not be real.

Number Math Jokes

I ordered from the local Chinese restaurant last night. My order consisted of a (23), a (13), a (31) and a (79).
*They tasted **odd. So,** I had to return them.*

Surgeon: Nurse! I have way too many patients! I do not know who to work on first!
*Nurse: It's quite simple. You should use the **order of the operations.***

Why don't people do mathematics in the jungle?
*Because, when you add together **(4+4 you get 8)**!*

Bob, Farmer Fred's sheepdog, was rounding the sheep up. When he was done with his task, he quickly ran over to Farmer Fred shouting "Farmer Fred, Farmer Fred.... I chased (40) sheep into the yard for you".
"(40) sheep?" after thinking about it Farmer Fred remarked. "I've only got (37)" "I know," says Bob. ***"I rounded them up"***

Kid: Father, can you aid me in finding the lowest of the common denominator in this math equation?
Father: They have not found that one? I was

74

searching for that number back when I went to school.

Geometry Math Jokes

Why do you not see math instructors on the beach?
They do not need the beach to divide the sin from the cosine to get a result of a tan.

If you have a pot of boiling water and you place it on the mountaintop, what do you have?
*A **high pot in use***

What do you call an angle that is crushed?
Rect-angle

What caused the Geometry instructor to stay home today??
*She had a broken **angle!!***

What is a cross between McDonalds and geometry?
*A **plain cheeseburger.***

What was said when the witch doctor removed the curse?
Hex a gon

What is the coldest triangle?
Ice sosceles triangles.

What do you call a professional grade tractor?
Pro-tractors

The (45/45/90) triangle was supposed to marry the (30/60/90) triangle today. Why is that?
*They were considered the **right** type of couple.*

Why did the angle get a loan?
*He was able to find a **cosign.***

Statistics Math Jokes

A mother with three kids and one on the way was sitting at the dinner table.
One dreary evening, the first child says to her Father: "Father, guess what I heard?" "What did you hear." "Mommies new baby will be Chinese!" "What?!"
*"Yea. I read in the newspaper **that by statistics every 4th child** born is Chinese..."*

Why did the statistics student rush through the junctions while driving his car?
Statistically, you are more likely to get killed in a junction than anywhere else. So, speeding through allows him to spend less time in the junction.

Why did the student drum on her algebra book?
*The class was studying **log rhythms**.*

George W. Bush delivered a speech in Algeria and informed them, "You know, I really regret that I will give this speech in English. I would really prefer to talk to you in your own language. *However, unfortunately, I was no good at **algebra...**"*

If you have (8) items, and then you add them (8x), the resulting number is (1,000). How is this done only using addition?
(1,000=888+88 +8 +8 +8)

What is the tiniest 3-digit palindrome that you can divide by (18)?
(252)

How many eggs can you add to an empty bucket?
***Only one can go into an empty bucket**. After adding in one that bucket, it is no longer an empty one.*

What store are you able to purchase a ruler at which is at least 3-ft long?
*The **yard** sale store*

Which coin will double in value if ½ of it is reduced?
half $.

What has 3-ft without toes?
*A **yardstick**.*

Why do diapers resemble $100 bills?
*You must **change** them*

What in your life goes up but doesn't come down?

Age

Why is the ear not more than 11-inches?
*Because then it is a **foot**.*

Two mothers sat down with two daughters at the table to devour pancakes for breakfast. They consumed three pancakes; with each person having a single pancake. Why is this possible?
*It was a **grandmother, mother, and daughter**.*

You're on a school bus. There are (10) people already on the bus. At the first school, (7) people get off. Then (2) people get on. At the next school, (2) people get off and (8) people go ahead to get on. At the last school, (4) people get off and (2) more people get on. At the bus depot, no one gets on or off. How many people are on the bus?
***(10)**. Because of the bus driver. And I said "people" not "children"*

Together Jake, John, and Joe weight (720) lbs. if John weighs (3x) as much as Jake and Jake weighs (1/2) as much as Joe. How much does each man weigh?
***720/ 6 tells us that Jake weighs 120lb., so Joes weight 240lb. and John weighs 360lb...** (consider $x + 2x + 3x = 720$).*

If you are sending (96) boxes to your friend. The shipping crate only holds (8) large boxes or (10) small boxes. How many boxes did the ship carry, if there are more of the large boxes than there are of the small boxes?
(7 * 8 = 56) +(4 *10 = **40) boxes, this means that there are a total of 11 cartons and a total of 96 boxes**

Diophantus's was young 1/6th of his life. His beard grew at 1/12th of his lifespan. He married after 1/7th of his lifespan. 5 years later, his had their son. The son lived for 1/2 as long as his father, Diophantus. Diophantus died 4 years before his son's death. How many years did Diophantus live?
Diophantus lived exactly 84 years.

Add the day and month to get the year and you have the sum-date.
What is the last sum-day of the century we are in?
The last one is **12+31=43, December 31, 2043.**

The amount of sum-days in the 21st century is??
365, since all days that are not in a leap year equal to a sum-date eventually

Why won't the dog drink the water with the ice cubes?
Because it was too cubed for him.

What is the 1st cow derivative?
Prime Ribs!

What value is there for the integral contour on the Western side of Europe?
0.
Why is this?
The poles can be found on the Eastern side of Europe!

What did one Ph.D. communicate to the other Ph.D. in math?
"Paper or plastic?"

What's the derivative of Amazon for the cost of shipping?
Amazon Prime!

Who works for the phone company and is polite?
An ***operator deferential***

What did Art Garfunkel use to find his rhythm?
An ***Algo rhythm***

What is commutative and purple?
grape abelian

Did you hear about the math teacher who was hot?
She ***derives all the pupils crazy.***

What cat is amazing at doing calculus?
The **lion tangent.**

The Calculus instructor was bad at baseball. Why?
He could ***fit curves better than he could hit them***.

What's is the same as an Axiom of Choice and also yellow?
Lemon Zorn's.

Why did the algebra students throw the bottle of sanitizer across the classroom?
They were **projectiles he was investigating**.

Why is the demand for the function of interpolation starting to get more expensive in order to compute it?
The **Law of Demand and Spline**

If you have in one hand (7) apples and in other (5) apples what do you have?
2 big hand

Do you want to know something odd?
1

What do you call a sea creature that knows addition?

*An **Octo plus**.*

What does a hungry math nerd snack on?
Gram crackers!

What do you call a boss that refuses to fire anyone?
*All talk and **no subtraction.***

Why can't you put (8) and (2) next to each other in math class?
*Because they do not **pay at(10)ention.***

How do you make Todd an odd number?
*Take the **T out of him**.*

Why do golfers put minus signs in front of their scores?
*Because **subtraction speaks louder than words.***

What's 1 + 1?
*A **math equation!***

Bob has (38) Candy Bars, he eats (30), what does he have now?
*Diabetes, **Bob has Diabetes.***

Why did 2 and 2 get in a box?
Because it was 4 (for) them!

There are thirty cows and (28) chickens. How many died?
10! 30 cows and 20 cows 8 chickens!!! get it?

There is a fine line between a **Numerator/Denominator.**

The best time on a clock is **6:30 hands down.**

Teacher: Can you locate the square root for a million.
*Student: I think that is so much **more radical?***

Teacher: Your behavior is kind of reminding me of the root squared for 2?
Student: Why?
*Teacher: It is **irrational, completely.***

Math Mistakes

The boss tried to belittle his employee because of a minor error in his math. Frustrated, she asked, "If I asked you for a bagel and you had (4) bagels how many would you have?"
The employee responded, **"If you asked me, I would still have (4) bagels."**

What did the baby tree exclaim when he finally saw his reflection in his mirrors?
Gee, I'm a tree

What will happen when you mix a pebble with a sphere?
rock and roll!

What is a protractor holding a fishing rod called?
An Angler!

What geometry shape will you find at a Starbucks?
The line.

What did the circle and square talk about?
Have I seen you around?

The students loved their trigonometry teacher. Why?

*He never gave any homework **as SIN ments.***

What's a math teachers favorite movie?
Trig Identity.

What did the mommy triangle say to the baby triangle?
*Stop being so **ILLUMI naughty!***

What are the similarities between people who are whiny and (3) points?
*They are both considered **co planers***

That slice of chocolate pie has how many grams of protein?
3.142

What was said by the complementary angle to the isosceles triangle?
Nice Legs

What is more than one L?
A Parallel

Why is the corner of the room so hot?
*Because it was **(90) degrees Fahrenheit!***

Do you do when it rains?
Coincide

Why were the triangles that were similar in weight, weighing themselves?
*They needed to find their **scales**.*

The circles did not invite the ellipses to come to his house for dinner, why is that?
*They were considered to be overly **eccentric**.*

Why is this geometry textbook consistently so unhappy?
Because has an extensive amount of problems that have no real answers.

The scalene triangle was so sad. Why?
He would never be able to turn right.

What makes Ms. Radian a great reporter?
*She is known for covering the story **from every angle**.*

When ellipses, circle, parabolas, and hyperbolas hang out for summer, where do they go?
Coney Island.

What was the reason why the chicken did not move to the opposite side of the inequality?
***The boundary line** was not able to be passed.*

When you cross a linebacker with a computer geek, what do you get?
A linear programmer.

When the Math teacher committed murder what did she do?
A sin!

What shape do you use to catch another person?
A trapezoid.

What is a small dog called?
An **acute one.**

How is the broken record defined?
Life is pointless, *no geometry and already a Decca-gone.*

Student: "I'm cold"
Math Teacher: "Then go to the corner!"
Student: "Why?"
Math Teacher: "Because it's 90 degrees!"

One day there was a queen and king who lived in a roundhouse. One morning their daughter was murdered. They interviewed everyone in the house to find who the murderer was. They asked their son and the two maids. One maid was sweeping the corners, one was dusting the bookshelf, and the brother was in his room. The queen asked the King who do you think killed our daughter? The king said, *"the maid sweeping the corners since this is a* **roundhouse***."*

Why was the y-intercept so terrifying to the student?
*She was worried about being stung by a **b**.*

What would be a hidden math term? BOLA-BOLA
Para bolas

What happens when you blend algebra class with the prom?
*The **quadratic becomes formal**.*

What made the number that was imaginary become red?
*It ran out of **eye medicine**.*

How did all the apples in the bowl know who they each were?
*They happen to be **relations to the core**.*

What caused the police to arrest the matrix?
***Their entry was illegal**.*

If a rodent has babies what is its name?
*A **quad-rat-ic parent***

What caused the local Doctor to send the expression to a psychiatrist?
He was totally irrational.

How can someone determine the number of protestors that will be present at the rally?
By using a ***function for radicals***.

A ***hyper boa*** is a snake that drank 3 cups of caffeinated coffee.

When you square a Ho you get?
Ho, Ho, Ho

How can you tell the enthusiasm of a factorial?
Because the exclamation is on point.

When people are taken at an ***absolute value*** they are considered negative.

Teacher: "What is three Q + seven Q?"
Student: "Ten Q"
Teacher: **"You're Welcome."**

Parent: Can you do your algebra homework?

Student: Sure, it was easy as a ***function to relations***.

Teacher: Why did you allow your parents to do the algebra homework I assigned you?
Student: *They understood parent **functions**, completely.*

Student: The Picasso must really understand algebra.
Parent: Why?
Student: **He probably did lots of factoring, he was a famous cubist.**

Everything about girls frightens me, Father. That is what caused me to fail my algebra test? What do girls have to do with algebra? **Because it has the word "bra" in it.**

Made in the USA
Las Vegas, NV
30 October 2022